D1412448

JOY RIDE

Sherri Duskey Rinker

illustrated by

Ana Ramírez González

Candlewick Press

IT'S THE THIRD DAY of summer vacation, and I've already tie-dyed two shirts, fancied up a boring old hat, and made a new outfit for Max.

I ask Mom if we have anything else I can spiff up.

"Joy, maybe you'd like to visit Granddad today?" she responds.

Mom says I'm a lot like Granddad: we're both always looking to tinker with something.

I ride my brother's old bike to Granddad's house.

"Mom says I need a summer

project," I tell Granddad.

He pulls out all sorts of

thingamajigs and whatchamacallits

and holds them up, one by one.

Each time he asks, "How 'bout this?"

Each time I shake my head.

It takes a long while.

But as soon as I see it, I know it's *perfect*.

I help Granddad pull it past
buckets and crates that fall and clank,
then through the rickety door.

Though it's bent and rusty, I get even more excited when I see it in the light. Like a plain shirt or an old hat, it's just wanting to be tinkered with and spiffed up.

Granddad scratches his head. "Well, she needs some work.
She hasn't been ridden in a good long while."

"You can fix her," I say. "I mean, can you? I mean, can we?"

"It'll be a lot of work," he says—but I can tell he's kind of excited, too.

"I'll help! And we can make it extra fancy!"

"Fancy, eh?" Granddad rubs his stubbly cheek. "Well, I don't know much about 'fancy,' but I s'pose you can be in charge of that part."

Next thing I know, we're at the hardware store, where everybody knows Granddad, and they say, "Hey there, Charlie!" when we walk in. We fill our basket with gizmos and gadgets and stuff for cleaning and stuff for decorating.

When it's time to pick the paint, Granddad lifts me up high so I can see all the colors.

I know right away.

We find the rest of the stuff we need over the next few days: rainbow streamers and a white wicker basket with flowers . . .

the perfect banana-shaped seat . . .

and material to cover it.

Granddad does most of the fixing, but I watch and help. It feels like it takes forever—especially when I have to ride my brother's boring old hand-me-down bike.

Finally, there's just one step left.

"This glue should hold 'em," Granddad says. And he helps me stick on the fancy bits, one by one, up and down the whole frame.

"Just right," I say as we fill in the last empty spaces.

And then it's done!

I get on and push off down the road. *Whirr!*

The wind blows against my face. *Whoosh!*

Rainbow streamers go *whippity-whip-whippity-whip-whip!*

The cards in my spokes say *tickety-tickety-tickety-tickety-tickety.*

I ring the bell: *ting-ting!*

Today, I'm not just Joy; I'm JOY!!!
The whole bike sparkles as I ride.

I ride and ride and ride and ride.
Whirr-whirr-whirr-whirr! JOY! JOY! JOY! JOY!

I can't wait to show everyone what we made, Granddad and me.

Sometimes friends are not very nice.

Sometimes strangers aren't either.

Just. Like. THAT:

No JOY. Just plain-old Joy.

Plus sad.

Plus MAD.

I don't think before I do it.

I ride up to the top of the hill and hop off.

Then, as hard as I can, I push the bike into the woods.

I walk home with a giant lump in my
throat that makes me feel like I can't swallow.

But I'm still mad.

Later, I ride the old hand-
me-down bike up the road.

The whole way, there's no music.

No *whippity-whip-whippity-whip-whip* from the rainbow streamers.

No *tickety-tickety-tickety-tickety-tickety* from the cards in my spokes.

No sparkling in the sun.

No basket. No bell. No tall, graceful handlebars.

No flowery banana-shaped seat.

But no more teasing, either.

It's better.
It's okay.
At least, it's the same.

I'm not mad anymore.
But I'm not happy, either.

On my way home, I stop at Granddad's house
and stare at the door for a long while.

Then I pedal home fast.

That night, I can't sleep.

"How's it going with that fancy bike of yours?"
Granddad asks the next day.

I have a twisty feeling inside when I lie.

"Fine," I say.

Granddad's brown eyes
look into my brown eyes.

When I go past the woods on
my way home, I try hard not to
think about the bike.

Instead, I think about the kids who teased me, all looking
pretty much the same—even my friends. Clothes, shoes, jackets,
backpacks, bikes. All alike. Nothing different. Nothing special.
Nothing fancy. Plain.

And right then, I know what
I need to do.

It takes a long time to get the bike out of the deep leaves and the twisty branches. It takes even longer to push it back up the steep hill to the road and down the long driveway to Granddad's house.

"What happened?" Granddad asks.

"It had an accident," I say.

He just looks at me. His brown eyes. My brown eyes.

"I mean, I made a mistake."

"Happens to the best of us," Granddad finally says.
"Looks like it'll take a good bit of work to
get 'er back in shape."

"Mom says you can fix anything," I say.

He laughs a little, and the twisty feeling
in my gut starts to unknot.

"Well, I reckon we can tinker
with it together—see if we can spiff
it back up. You'll have
to be in charge of the
fancying, though."

I nod.

And we both smile—
a wide smile. Exactly the
same.

And once again . . .

I'm JOY.

For Andie, on your path to finding joy. Keep pedaling. You'll get there.
SDR

This book is for my parents and my sister,
who taught me how to ride my bike in circles on a tiny back patio
and then had to reteach me how to go straight. I love you!
ARG

First edition 2022

Library of Congress Catalog Card Number 2021946796

ISBN 978-1-5362-0774-3

22 23 24 25 26 27 APS 10 9 8 7 6 5 4 3 2 1

Printed in Humen, Dongguan, China

This book was typeset in Rockwell.

The illustrations were created digitally.

Candlewick Press

99 Dover Street

Somerville, Massachusetts 02144

www.candlewick.com